big & SMALL

Original Korean text by Ki-seon Jang
Illustrations by Eun-yeong Choi
Korean edition © Aram Publishing

This English edition published by big & SMALL in 2017
by arrangement with Aram Publishing
English text edited by Joy Cowley
English edition © big & SMALL 2017

Distributed in the United States and Canada by
Lerner Publishing Group, Inc.
241 First Avenue North
Minneapolis, MN 55401 U.S.A.
www.lernerbooks.com

ISBN: 978-1-925235-38-8
Printed in Korea

The Farting Princess

Written by Ki-seon Jang
Illustrated by Eun-yeong Choi
Edited by Joy Cowley

Long ago, there was a princess
who had a gassy problem.
Boom! Boom! Pop! Pop!
She had stinky farts that
sounded like thunder.

The princess wanted to marry.
Many princes came to see her,
but they ran away when the princess farted.

The King was worried. "What is
wrong with my daughter?" he sighed.
"She must be under a magic spell."

One day, a young man came to see the princess.

The princess farted very loudly.
Boom! Boom! Pop! Pop!
It made a terrible smell, but the young man
did not run away.

9

The king talked to the young man.
"If you can save my daughter
from this terrible magic spell,
I will give you anything you want."

The young man replied,
"I will try to help the princess."

cheese ham eggs

pizza beans

12

The young man watched
what the princess ate
for several days.

Then the young man went to the king.
"Allow me to cook for the princess
for a week," said the young man.

"You may do so," replied the king.

The day after the young man
cooked for the princess,
she farted a little less.
By the end of that week,
she barely farted at all.
The awful smell was finally gone.

Some foods don't cause as much gas. They include:
- lean meats
- grapes and berries
- spinach
- whole grains

The young man said to the king,
"There was no magic spell.
The princess's old diet caused
the problem."

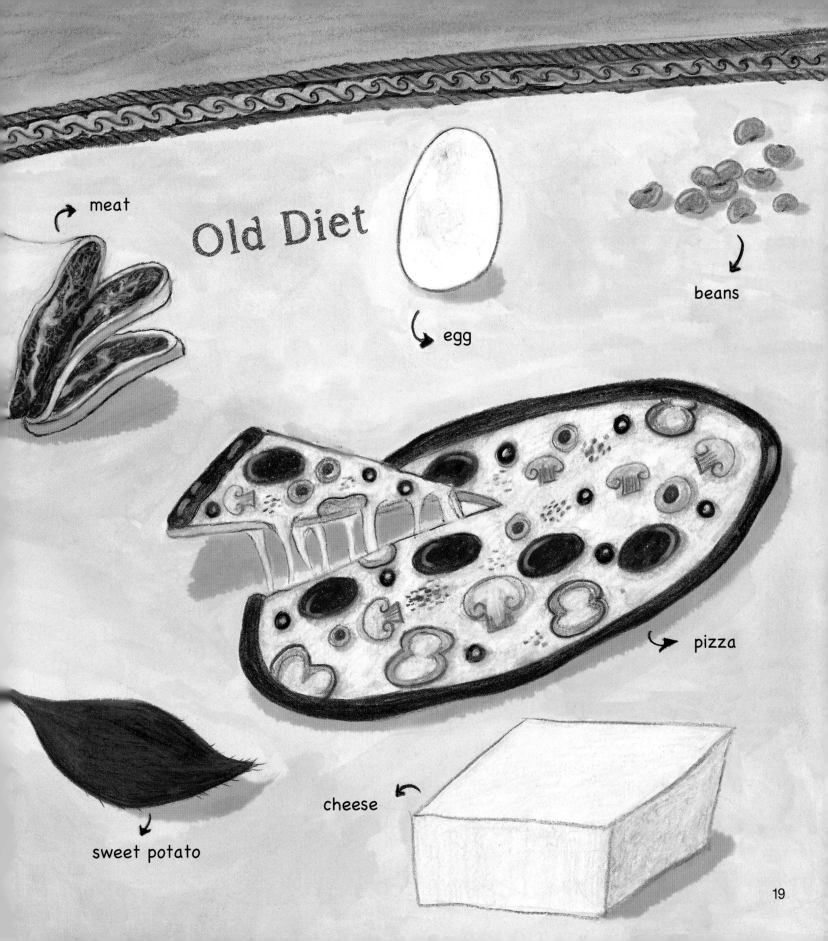

Old Diet

meat

egg

beans

pizza

sweet potato

cheese

Food mixed with saliva moves through the esophagus.

The young man explained, "Food goes from your mouth, through your esophagus, and into your stomach. It is broken down into smaller pieces in your stomach. Then it moves through your small and large intestines."

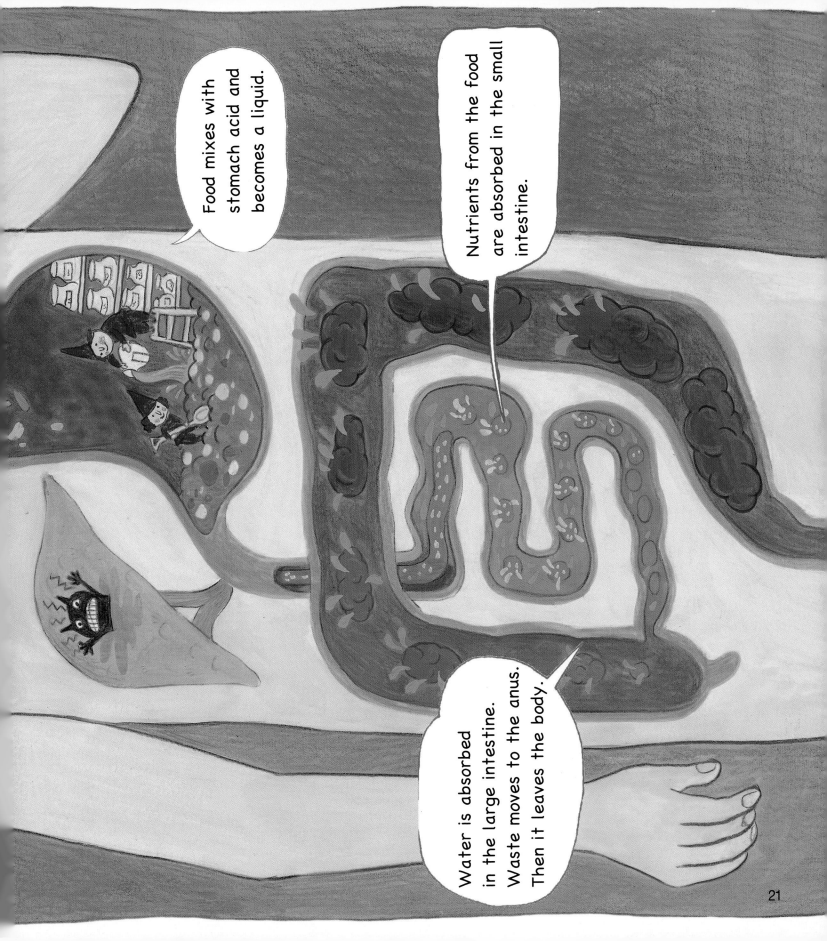

The young man said to the king, "Everybody farts. Some gas comes from the air we breathe. Other gas is made while we digest food."

"Why were my daughter's farts so loud and smelly?" asked the king.

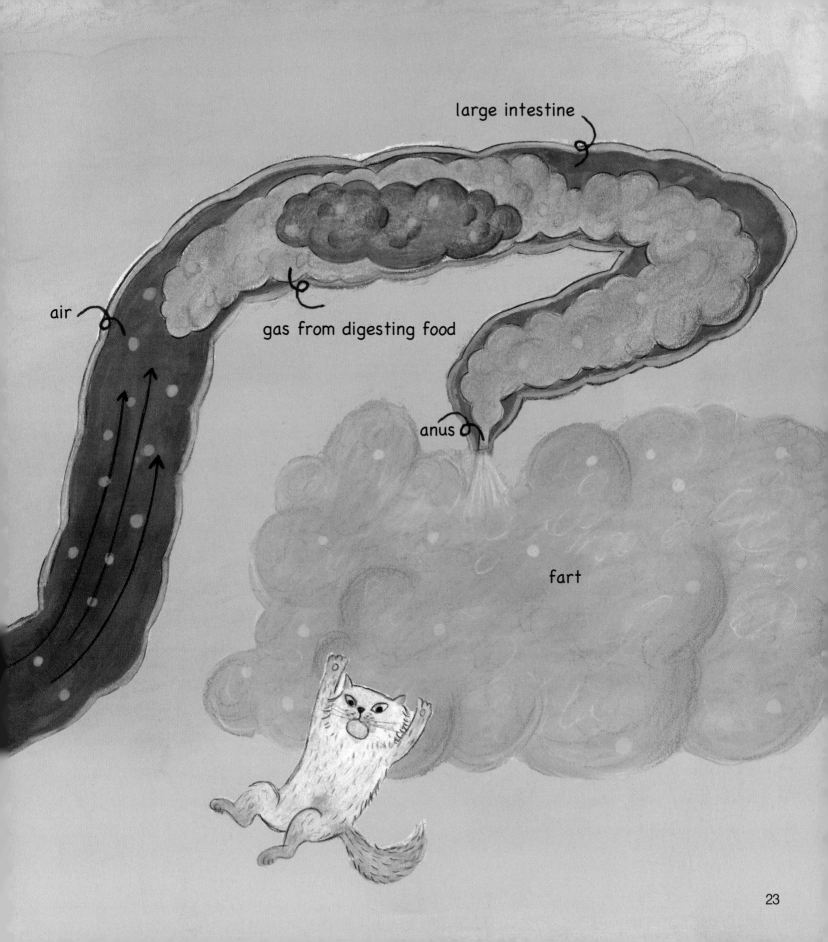

large intestine

air

gas from digesting food

anus

fart

cheese

"There are two reasons for that," said the young man. "The food you eat is important. Eggs, beans, cheese, meat, and fried foods cause more gas. If you eat in a hurry, more air enters your mouth. That can make you gassy too."

"Ah!" said the king. "So it was her eating habits that caused her gassy problem."

"Yes, your majesty," said the young man. "I cooked her foods that don't cause so much gas and I asked the princess to eat slowly."

The king said to the young man,
"You must always cook for my daughter.
Perhaps she can marry the next prince
who comes to visit."

The princess smiled and said,
"Father, my prince is here,"
as she looked at the young man.

The young man's face turned red.
It was true. He was in love.
He wanted to marry the princess
and live happily ever after.

The Farting Princess

A beautiful princess can't stop farting. Everybody farts, but some foods make people really gassy. They have loud and smelly farts. Eating quickly causes farting too. But with the right diet and eating habits, farting is not a problem.

Let's think!

What food made the princess fart?

Which foods don't cause much gas?

Where does food go from your mouth?

What happens to food in your stomach?

Let's do!

Make a fart journal. Write down how many times you pass gas in a week. Record what you eat each day too. At the end of the week, look at your results.
What foods made you most gassy?
What foods were low-gas?